Brimming with creative inspiration, how-to projects, and useful information to enrich your everyday life, Quarto Knows is a favourite destination for those pursuing their interests and passions. Visit our site and dig deeper with our books into your area of interest: Quarto Creates, Quarto Cooks, Quarto Homes, Quarto Lives, Quarto Drives, Quarto Explores, Quarto Gifts, or Quarto Kids.

First published in 2018 by Frances Lincoln Children's Books, an imprint of The Quarto Group.
The Old Brewery, 6 Blundell Street, London N7 9BH, United Kingdom.
T (0)20 7700 6700 F (0)20 7700 8066 www.QuartoKnows.com

A catalogue record for this book is available from the British Library.

ISBN 978-1-78603-067-2

The illustrations were created digitally
Set in Helsing

Published by Rachel Williams and Jenny Broom
Designed by Zoë Tucker
Edited by Katie Cotton
Production by Jenny Cundill

Manufactured in Shenzhen, China RD 102017

9 8 7 6 5 4 3 2 1

For all my relations
With special thanks
to James and Celia
D.C

For my Mom, with love
O.L

Dawn Casey
& Oamul Lu

Held in Love

Frances Lincoln
Children's Books

*Within the universe,
a galaxy is glowing.*

Within the galaxy,
the world is turning.

Within the world,
the hills are rolling.

Within the hills,
a village is nestling.

Within the village,
a home is resting.

Within the home,
a mother is reading.

Within her arms,
a child is held.
And, on her lips,
a blessing.

May
your
feet
skip

and leap.

May your hands
work and play...

...*give and receive.*

*May your ears listen,
and hear the singing...*

and the silence.

May your lips smile.
May your belly laugh.

And when tears flow,

*may peace
follow.*

And may your eyes look to the stars

and know...

...that you are held in the arms
of the universe,

held in love.